THE HOUSE

Rachel McLean writes thrillers that make your pulse race and your brain tick. Originally a self-publishing sensation, she has sold millions of copies digitally, with massive success in the UK, and a growing reach internationally. She is the author of the Dorset Crime novels and the spin-off McBride & Tanner series and Cumbria Crime series. In 2021, she won the Kindle Storyteller Award with *The Corfe Castle Murders* and her books regularly hit No 1 in the Bookstat ebook chart on launch.

Joel Hames is a Lancashire-based writer of crime fiction, and the editor of million-selling books across multiple genres. Joel's own works include the Dead North series featuring lawyer Sam Williams, and the psychological thriller *The Lies I Tell*. Most recently, he has been working with titan of crime fiction Rachel McLean on the hugely successful Cumbria Crime series.

ALSO BY RACHEL MCLEAN AND JOEL HAMES

Cumbria Crime series

The Harbour
The Mine
The Cairn
The Barn
The Lake
The Wood
...and more to come

CUMBRIA CRIME NOVELLA

THE HOUSE

Copyright © 2025 by Rachel McLean and Joel Hames

All rights reserved.

No part of this book may be reproduced in any form or by any electronic or mechanical means, including information storage and retrieval systems, without written permission from the author, except for the use of brief quotations in a book review.

This is a work of fiction. Names, characters, businesses, places, events and incidents are either the products of the author's imagination or used in a fictitious manner. Any resemblance to actual persons, living or dead, or actual events is purely coincidental.

Ackroyd Publishing

ackroydpublishing.com

Printed and bound by CPI Group (UK) Ltd, Croydon, CR0 4YY

CHAPTER ONE

WEDNESDAY

Bobby Silver pushed through the door and stood, dripping onto the carpet, waiting for her eyes to adjust.

It was shit out. Worse than shit. Like someone had thrown a bucket of ice and water over the country, and most of it had landed on Cumbria.

Still, no surprise. Not for someone who knew the county. And at least it was dry inside the Henry Bessemer.

She spotted Miles, the overhead lights picking out the lines, scars, and bruises of thirty years' work at the port. He was in the corner of the pub, where the music was quietest.

Stacey was with him; no missing those earrings.

Bobby smiled and made for the bar. It was busy, a night for gathering inside, shutting out the cold and pretending it wasn't there. It took her nearly five minutes to get a pint of the guest bitter, served by a young barman she didn't recognise. He peered around in confusion before she pointed him to the tap.

Everything was different these days. Bobby Silver had lived and worked around here all her life. She'd been drinking in the local pubs for more than forty years – they started early in Workington – and she knew the people the same way she knew the roads, without having to think about it.

But for the last year, there'd been a sense that things had changed too much. That the ground she'd been sure of could move at any moment, sending her...

Stupid. Stupid to think like that. Victor was dead, and it was terrible. He'd been her best friend. The closest thing she'd had to a son. But it had been a year, or near enough.

She had to move on.

Bobby made her way through the press of people, clutching her glass, until she reached her friends. They'd found a spot to one side, with a ledge she could balance her beer on.

"'Right?" asked Miles.

"'Right," Bobby replied. Stacey was watching her. Bobby smiled and shrugged. "Not bad, anyway."

She couldn't hide things from people who knew her like this lot did.

"Next week, isn't it?" asked Miles, catching on.

Bobby sighed and gave him a nod. "Next Thursday. You're coming, right?"

"Wouldn't miss it."

Memorial drinks. It would be a year since they'd found Victor's body. They'd be gathering in the Henry Bessemer, everyone who wanted to, the people who'd worked alongside him. And they'd be drinking themselves stupid.

No more than Victor deserved.

She reached into her pocket and pulled out a tub of Vaseline, applying it to her lips before putting it beside her half-empty pint on the ledge.

CHAPTER ONE

Stacey smirked. "Still using that shit, are you?"

Bobby raised an eyebrow. "We don't all have your miracle skin, Stacey."

Stacey shrugged.

"And," Bobby added, "some of us can't be arsed spending a fortune on moisturisers and pretending it's all natural."

Stacey opened her mouth to object. Bobby raised the eyebrow further. Beside her, Miles was trying not to laugh, his mouth full of beer.

"It's not a fortune," said Stacey. "I just have a regime. Look after myself."

"Don't worry about it," Bobby replied. "We can't all look like Miles here."

"Hey!" said Miles.

"It's a compliment, lad. The thousand-year-old man look suits you. Take the win."

Miles took a long gulp of lager. Bobby turned to survey the crowd, seeking out more familiar faces at the bar. When she turned back, Aaron Keyes was approaching.

"Bloody hell," she said, pointing him out to the others.

"Cop's coming," observed Miles.

"He's OK," Bobby replied. "Victor liked him."

"That he did," Miles nodded. "But then, Victor liked you. Great man, Victor, but you can't say he had good taste in friends."

"Fuck off," said Bobby, laughing, as Aaron joined them.

"Alright?" he asked. He held a glass of something clear. Lemonade, knowing him.

"Great," Bobby replied. Miles just nodded. Stacey gave Aaron one of those dirty winks she was famous for, and the cop blinked and took half a step back.

DS Aaron Keyes. Stacey knew he was gay, didn't she?

"Miserable out there," Aaron said, pulling off a damp coat and folding it over one arm. "Feels like it's been like this for weeks."

"Months," Miles observed.

Bobby took another drink and applied more Vaseline to her lips. She looked up to see Aaron eyeing her.

"Wind on the docks dries your skin up," she explained. She watched his gaze pass over Stacey's expensively smoothed face and come to rest on Miles, who shrugged. It was alright for him. He was happy looking like a dried-up riverbed.

"Listen," said Aaron. "Any of you lot heard of a man called Josh McKenzie?"

Bobby forced her face to remain in a neutral frown. *Don't move.* Not a single muscle.

Not a fucking nerve.

"Sorry," said Stacey. "Not me."

Miles shook his head. Bobby slipped into what she hoped was an easy smile.

"Nope," she said.

Aaron was watching her.

Was there something careful in that look? Had he asked her because he already knew?

Or was it just coincidence?

"Why?" she asked. "He owe you money?"

"No." Aaron smiled and looked away.

She forced herself to breathe again. He had no idea that she knew McKenzie, that he worked with her. For her, really. That he was one small part in the secret little operation that had quietly made a very wealthy woman of her. Aaron Keyes didn't know a thing.

It made you paranoid, this business.

She took a deep gulp of bitter. To think. To recover.

Aaron was talking again.

"Someone slashed the poor bastard's throat and dumped him in Ennerdale Water," he said.

All the beer she hadn't got round to swallowing ended up on the floor. "Fuck."

All three of them were staring at her, but then, you would stare at someone who'd just spat a quarter of a pint on the floor.

And spitting a quarter of a pint of beer on the floor wasn't suspicious, not after hearing that. Even if she didn't know McKenzie.

"Sorry," she added. "Didn't mean to do that. What you asking us for, Aaron?"

"I don't know." He shrugged, and she eyed him.

Was it true? McKenzie, dead? She hadn't heard from him in a while, but she tended to deal directly with Cummings. He dealt with McKenzie. McKenzie dealt with the rest. She didn't much like dealing with any of them, and Cummings was the worst of the bunch, but still, it was easier that way.

But why had Aaron asked them? Was he hoping she'd give something away? She could sense him becoming uncomfortable under her gaze.

"I'm trying to figure out if he had any connection with the port," he explained.

"He work there?" asked Miles. "Don't recognise the name, but there's enough of us."

Aaron shook his head. "He worked at the Bassenthwaite Manor Hotel."

So he knew that, then. How much else did he know?

Stacey gave a whistle. Bobby was shaking her head, but Aaron wasn't looking at her. Not obviously, at least.

Trying to still the tremor in her hands, and hoping it wouldn't come through in her voice, she lifted her glass and drank again. "Do me a favour, Aaron," she said.

He turned to her.

"Will you stop being a copper, just for a minute?"

A shrug. "I'll give it a go. But since I've got to head back to the station in a bit, it won't be easy." He lifted his own glass, finished his drink, and checked his watch. "Come on, then. My round."

He was gone for five minutes, long enough for Bobby to establish that Stacey and Miles, at least, didn't suspect a thing. She could tell. Didn't have to ask; it was in their body language.

If they'd been watching her when Aaron had been talking, they'd have seen it in her, but their attention had been on him.

By the time he was back, moving through the crowd with a tray laden with three full pint glasses and another lemonade, Bobby felt more herself.

"You coming next week?" she asked.

He frowned. "What's next week?"

He didn't know. How could he?

"Drinks," she said. "For Victor. Here. Next Thursday at two."

He nodded, frowning. "Shit," he said. "It's a year, right?"

"One year on Thursday, yeah."

Not a year since he'd died. No one knew when he'd died. Not exactly. A year since they'd found his body.

"Shit," he repeated. "Sorry. I'll try. Supposed to be—"

"Working, yeah," she said. "Don't worry. I know you'll come if you can."

It felt grubby. Using Victor's death to change the subject. But she had no choice.

Aaron's lemonade was empty. He was checking his watch again.

A murder investigation. It wasn't like he could swan around doing nothing while the rest of them figured out who'd killed McKenzie.

But how the fuck was McKenzie dead?

"Got to run," said Aaron. "See you if I can."

"I hope so," Bobby told him.

He reached out and held the top of her arm. "I mean it," he said. "He was a good man."

Victor Parlick had been a good man. Unlike Josh McKenzie, who'd had his throat slashed and been dumped in Ennerdale Water. McKenzie hadn't been a good man, and the world would be a better place without him.

But who'd killed him?

And would they be coming for Bobby next?

CHAPTER TWO

THURSDAY

The village shop was less a shop, more the front room of a cottage on the closest thing they had to a main road. Mrs Gillespie, whose husband had died not long after Bobby had moved here, had found that with no one to look after, she had time to do what she wanted. Which was to fill her kitchen with cans and odd little items and sell them to whoever happened to drop in.

Most days, that was nobody. But Bobby made a habit of stopping by with the dog. It was good to support a local business. And besides, she'd run out of Vaseline.

"Come on, Taylor," she called. The shop was just a few minutes' walk away. But the dog was sitting in the snow, staring at her with big, reproachful eyes.

"Come on."

The dog had come from the rescue centre, eighteen months old, beaten and scared. It had been hard getting her to trust people again. Not to just slink about the place trying not to be noticed. Times like now, Bobby wondered whether

CHAPTER TWO

it had been worth it. An obedient dog wouldn't be such a pain.

Maybe she should have driven. The Honda didn't mind the snow.

But she'd wanted the walk. And Taylor had needed it.

"Taylor!" she snapped, and the dog rose reluctantly to her feet. It was Stacey who'd named the dog, insisting the long-haired dachshund was the canine spit of the global superstar. Bobby couldn't see it herself, but she'd been stuck for a name, so Taylor it was. The dog didn't seem to mind. Slowly, the two of them approached the shop.

Mrs Gillespie was as grumpy as usual. Why she'd opened a business that involved contact with the public was anyone's guess.

"S'pose you'll be wanting that weird stuff again, Mrs Silver," she said.

Bobby nodded. "Horrible weather, isn't it?"

"Ah, you city folk, you don't know what horrible weather is."

Bobby suppressed a smile. She was from Workington. If that made her 'city folk', Christ alone knew what the people from Carlisle were.

She waited while Mrs Gillespie opened cupboards and drawers, even though she knew the old woman would find the Vaseline in the same place she always found it, on the top shelf in the cupboard nearest the door. She'd mentioned it once, and the woman had glared at her with such venom she hadn't done it again.

"Here it is. Godawful nonsense. What d'you use this for?"

"I work at the port, Mrs Gillespie. It dries out my lips. I use this..."

The old woman wasn't listening. She might as well have explained that the dog liked to eat the stuff for all the response she'd have got. And the dog, meanwhile, was on as tight a lead as Bobby could manage, and whining to get out.

Fine. They'd get out.

She tried Cummings on the way back. If anyone knew what had happened to McKenzie, he would. But Cummings wasn't answering, just like he hadn't answered last night or all morning.

She didn't like it.

The burners they all used had basic voicemail capability, so she left a message.

"I don't know if you've heard about McKenzie," she said, "but you need to call me back and tell me what's going on. And while you're at it, answer the phone when I call. You can't still be on shift. Lying low's one thing. Avoiding me is something different."

She ended the call and turned to Taylor.

"That man is a useless piece of shit."

The dog looked up at her with what she could have sworn was agreement.

The weather turned as they headed back, from bad to near-apocalyptic. The cold bit like a knife, and the wind was one she could hear, not just bouncing off the fells but inside her head. By the time they made it back inside, Taylor was looking less pop icon, more glam rock star after an electric shock.

"Bugger off," said a voice as the door closed.

"Bugger off yourself," Bobby replied, and heard the familiar squawk in response.

Teaching Taylor to stick up for herself had been hard. Teaching Freddie to swear hadn't even been something she'd consciously chosen to do. But parrots had a way of picking up the things you didn't want them to. Like children, apparently. And 'Bugger off' was now Freddie's greeting for anyone entering the house.

Cummings finally called back an hour later, when Bobby and Taylor were steaming by the fire and Freddie was loose from his cage, circling the room and looking as disdainful as ever.

"Who is this?" she asked. It was Cummings's number, this week's burner, but it paid to check.

"It's me," he replied in that familiar whine.

"Cummings."

"Yeah. I got your message."

"Bugger off, Cummings," said Freddie, perching briefly by the fire.

"What's going on?" Bobby asked, at the same time.

"Yeah, it's true."

"What's true?"

"About McKenzie."

"Come on, Cummings. What's happened?"

"Bugger off, Cummings," said Freddie.

"What was that?"

"Nothing." She didn't have the energy to explain. "What's happened to McKenzie?"

"He's dead." Cummings's tone was flat. Matter-of-fact.

"Who did it?" she asked. "Is it Carter's people?"

"Zoe Finch's lot are looking at it."

"That's not what I asked."

"Look, I don't know, do I? I'm just a fucking Uniform, Bobby. Your mate probably knows better than I do."

"Who's that?"

"The queer one. Keyes."

Bobby closed her eyes and counted to ten. She could feel the air move around her as Freddie circled the room.

Bugger off, Cummings.

"I can hardly ask Aaron Keyes, can I?" she said.

There was a silence, broken by Freddie, this time shouting, "Wipe your feet, Taylor." The more Bobby said something, the more the damn parrot repeated it. The dog glanced up in what looked like confusion.

Poor Taylor.

"Who the fuck's Taylor?" asked Cummings.

"My dog," Bobby replied.

"Who's telling your dog to wipe its feet?"

"My parrot." There were other things she wanted to say, more important things, but she kept her mouth shut.

It didn't pay to antagonise Cummings, or his superiors.

"Look, it'll all work out," he said. "Shame about McKenzie, but we'll make it up."

She grunted a half-hearted agreement.

"In the meantime," he continued, "don't call me unless you have to. People are watching."

"Watching you?"

A laugh. "Watching everyone. So don't call."

"I won't, if you keep me informed. I can't be learning that one of my own team's been murdered from a cop in a fucking pub."

"Yeah, well, you can chill out, 'cause there won't be any more of that," he replied, ending the call.

"Shame," she said, into dead air. Cummings was probably the only one left. If someone took him out, it wouldn't be much of a loss. It wasn't like she needed the money. Not now. She could wind it all down. Live on what she had and what she picked up from her actual job.

CHAPTER TWO

"They're all pricks," she said. "The lot of them."

"All pricks," agreed Freddie, and for a second, she almost believed that he understood. All pricks. Carter and his thugs and his tame cop. Her own tame cop, Cummings. McKenzie had been no better. The others they'd picked up – she'd felt some guilt when she'd heard about the student. And again with the CSI. They'd died doing her work. They hadn't been the best of people, but they hadn't deserved that.

She should never have done it. Never got involved with any of them. But then...

She looked around the room. Through the open hallway to the huge glass front door. The track, snaking its way down to the road.

This was why she'd done it. This, and to get one over on Carter and his friends. She wouldn't change it.

She grabbed her tablet and pulled up a contact. A minute later, the screen was filled with the big, craggy head of Miles.

"I'm bored," she said.

He nodded. *Lonely*, she meant, and he knew it.

"You shouldn't be living up there by yourself in Bleak House," he told her.

The name had been Victor's idea, who'd only ever seen it in winter, when it could be pretty bloody bleak with the fields hidden under feet of snow and the wind beating at the old stone walls. She'd lied, of course. None of them knew about her operation. As far as they knew, she'd only been able to afford the place thanks to an obscure family inheritance, which made the name all the more appropriate.

"Drink?" she suggested.

"Drink," agreed Miles.

By the time she returned from the kitchen, beer in hand, Miles's face was obscured by a large glass of red wine.

He liked his red wine, did Miles.

"The last of the Chateauneuf," he told her.

She'd bought it for him. A case, six bottles, forty quid a pop, a few months back. Out of the inheritance, she'd told him.

"Cheers," he said.

"Cheers," she replied. "To Victor."

"To Victor."

She still missed him. She still wasn't over his death.

Would she ever be?

CHAPTER THREE

FRIDAY

By Friday morning, the wind had eased.

It was worse here at the port, the low flat expanse of sea no obstacle as it rushed in from the west, turning as it met the fells and slamming into her from the other side. Bobby knew about land breezes and sea breezes and laughed with the others at the word *breeze*. Nothing pummelling at her this week could be described as a *breeze*.

"Back up," she shouted into her radio, like she always did. Even when the wind had eased, she had to shout.

Stacey was driving her forklift, one of half a dozen circling the huge containers below. Stacey on one, Miles on another, then Barney and Ellen and Shiv and Liam a little further back. Those four were younger, their skin less scoured by the salt.

"What's up, boss?" she heard Miles say. He only ever called her that in front of her crew.

"Change of plan," she explained.

A phone call from the office had just come through. The cargo they were moving would have to stay where it was.

Other things needed doing, sooner. It wouldn't be drugs: there were only three crews that worked that side of the business, none of them in Bobby's team.

Not drugs. Not people. Probably just logs.

Always fucking logs. She watched them running through the port, an endless chain of wood, and wondered how there were any trees left in the world. All she saw all day, and then at night, too, dreams full of timber.

But then Victor had died, and her dreams filled with him instead.

An hour later she was sitting with Shiv sipping coffee that was already turning cold before she'd even taken her first sip.

"Seen this?" Shiv threw over the local paper she'd been reading.

It was there on the front page. *Local Man Found Dead in Beauty Spot.*

"Fucking hell," said Bobby. She didn't want Shiv knowing that she already knew.

Local Man Found Dead in Beauty Spot. It didn't say much. A chef, the article said he was. Chef, blackmailer, dealer, all-round piece of shit. *Suspicious circumstances* only made the third paragraph, with police appealing for information.

They weren't the only ones.

Beauty spot. Bobby had been there, years ago. She'd sat smoking and throwing back cans of beer with the lads on their bikes and the girls wearing bikinis in March. In the Lake District. Even then she'd known she was different.

People wouldn't be having picnics in that spot for a while.

She turned the page, and found herself reading another

CHAPTER THREE

story about another murder. A bit more detail this time, but this murder was old, as far as they went. Weeks. Maybe months.

A woman at the Bridge Inn. Strangled. Husband's prints on the door handle; they were smart, Aaron Keyes and his mates. He'd just been sentenced: life, obviously, fifteen years' tariff.

She looked back across the table, ready to share her thoughts with Victor, but he wasn't there, of course. Instead Shiv had her hand out, waiting for something.

"Come on, Bobby."

The paper. She'd only passed it over to show her the front page.

"Sorry, love." Bobby took a swig from her coffee and grimaced. Behind her the door opened and Stacey slid in, slipping her fags and lighter into her pocket and coughing.

She caught sight of the paper and nodded. "That the one Aaron was talking about the other day?" she said.

Bobby nodded. *That's the one.* But there were getting to be too many of them lately.

An hour later she was on a different cargo: plastics. She had her usual crew, which meant 'plastics' were legal. Small boxes, handle with care, but lots of them. She had to concentrate with a cargo like that, which was fine. It took her mind off the cold, amongst other things.

"Take five," she said, and the team melted away like ghosts. She smiled; *can't blame them.*

"You OK?"

Bobby looked up to see Miles, rolling one of his *you-shouldn't-smoke-that-here* specials. They'd given up on the drug testing when they realised just how many people they'd have to fire.

"Fuck's sake, Miles. Could be anyone about."

He shrugged. "What they gonna do?"

She shook her head. *Too dangerous.* "Just bugger off."

He grinned and slipped away.

She turned to look out past the ship. She couldn't see much today, not the turbines, or the tubs that moved between them like busy ants. She couldn't see the other cargo coming in and going out, all those forests. And she couldn't see what was hiding in the undergrowth: drugs, guns, people.

The people. That was what had done it for her. She'd held her nose and taken the money, for the drugs. She'd tried not to think about the guns.

But the people were different. She could tell if they knew, by the way they walked, by their expressions. Most of them tired and stiff and cold, and maybe a bit scared, but still expecting a warm home and a good job at the end of the journey.

And then, the ones shivering from more than just cold. The ones whose looks were more furtive, both careful and resigned. The ones who'd figured it out on the way over.

They were cargo, too. Only worth whatever Carter's mates would pay for them.

Fuck Carter. Fuck all of them. Bobby had set up her little operation and stolen what she could to get away from it all, because it wasn't like she could express her concerns to Myron Carter.

Bobby wasn't a religious woman. But after Neil Colvin and Huz Mahmoud, she was going to hell. They'd still be alive if she hadn't roped them in.

She heard footsteps and looked up.

Myron Carter was sauntering along the wharfside like he

owned not just the Port of Workington but the whole of bloody Cumbria.

Beside him, the tame cop. The one she hated even more than Carter. She'd toyed with the idea of telling Aaron, but how could she? Not without giving herself away.

They saw her at the same time. Carter gave her a sharp little nod. The cop narrowed his eyes. The air had turned even colder.

They knew. This was one of those little walk-pasts, the same thing that had done for Victor. *This one. You sure? I'm sure.*

Bobby felt a lump rise in her throat.

She turned away, focused her attention on the crew, making its way back. Trying to calm her breathing.

She glanced round to see Carter and the cop walking away, not turning back.

Maybe they don't know.

If they did, she'd be dead already. But still: they scared her shitless.

CHAPTER FOUR

SATURDAY

"Answer the bloody phone," Bobby said after the beep.

"Bugger off, Cummings," said the bird.

At least Freddie had the right name. Bobby had been calling him all morning, cursing that name. Freddie would be repeating it for weeks.

The snow was coming down again, so she'd stayed in and heated some soup for lunch. She had a meal for one in the fridge, ready for tea, a decent chilli con carne that would go nicely with a cold lager. But she wouldn't enjoy it. Not if Cummings didn't call her back.

She'd been worrying since yesterday, since seeing Carter and the cop at the Port. Since she'd heard about McKenzie. And now Cummings wasn't answering the phone.

Something's happened.

By early afternoon it had stopped snowing and the wind had dropped, but Taylor still didn't want to go out. They took a short stroll around the back, along the track into the woods. Usually Taylor loved it here, darting off into the trees like a hunting dog that had spotted a hare. But now she stayed by

Bobby's side, belly in the snow, ears flat to her head, sniffing the air and repeatedly turning as if she'd heard something.

"What is it, girl?" Bobby asked.

The dog just looked at her, mute. The parrot was as annoying as a toddler most of the time, but sometimes, she just wanted someone to speak.

They made their way back and sat in front of the fire, warming up while the news played out on the TV. War, famine, death, politicians. Bobby tried one more time. It rang eight times before switching to voicemail.

"Fuck's sake, Cummings," she muttered. "Just call me back."

Something had happened. She reached into her pocket, smeared Vaseline on her lips, and slid it back into her pocket.

She switched over to a movie, a comedy action thing she'd seen before and enjoyed, but she couldn't relax.

"This is shit," she said.

"Bugger off," agreed Freddie.

Taylor looked sadly at them, then returned to staring out of the window. Bobby returned her attention to the TV, where the villain was taking what had to be a fifth bullet to the stomach, none of which had even slowed him down.

"They need better bullets," she said, just as Taylor gave a sharp little bark.

"What is it?" Bobby asked.

Taylor got up from where she was lying on the rug in front of the fire and ran to the kitchen, then back through the living room and hallway, past the stairs to the big glass front door. Then back again.

Bobby felt the hairs on the back of her neck prickle. "What is it?"

"Bugger off," said Freddie.

On the TV, the villain was finally down. It had taken a grenade, though, and he was still moving, albeit slowly. She hit mute and strained her ears.

Nothing.

And then a moment later, the sound of an engine. Getting louder.

"Shit," she said.

From where she sat, Bobby had a good view through the front door of the track leading up to the house. It was one of the reasons she liked this house. But the weather had turned again, the snowfall obscuring the landscape. She didn't see it until it was almost at the house.

A Jeep. A green Jeep.

Expensive. But then, some of the farmers round here did well for themselves. And a Jeep was all kinds of practical.

But had she seen that Jeep before?

It moved past the front door, and stopped. Bobby got up, went to the window at the side, and saw them.

Two figures. One taller than the other, faces obscured. Both in boiler suits and balaclavas, climbing down from the Jeep.

"Shit."

"Shit," agreed Freddie.

The figures moved to the back of the car. The boot opened.

She had to move. But where?

Her brain wouldn't turn. It wouldn't tell her what to do.

She watched as one of the figures reached into the boot. Both hands. Gloved. Each one coming out holding a lump of dull metal.

Shit.

Bobby finally moved. She was at the front door before

she knew it, but they'd beaten her there. One of them, standing there, a grin clearly visible through the black fabric.

She didn't reckon she knew this one. Couldn't even tell if it was a man or a woman. The taller one was familiar, the way he'd walked, the calm, unhurried manner in which he'd opened the boot and reached inside. But this one was new.

The new one was pointing a gun at her.

The door was locked. Bobby knew it was locked. It was always locked.

"Shit," she said, out loud.

The door was locked. But the door was made of glass. And the person in the balaclava was holding a gun.

She ran back into the living room. Through the window at the side she could see the other one moving round to the back of the house. Calm. Unhurried.

"Bastard," she said.

"Bugger off," replied Freddie.

Taylor had stopped running around and was crouched in a corner, shaking.

How did the dog know? Could she smell Bobby's fear? Bobby stopped and looked around, then made for the kitchen.

She stopped again.

She'd come in that way, an hour earlier. Her and Taylor.

She'd left the back door unlocked.

She froze, ears straining again, this time for the sound of a handle turning, a door opening.

Nothing.

And nothing she could do. No solution. No way out. Freddie was flapping gently on his perch. Taylor was still shaking.

The animals. She couldn't let anything happen to the animals.

Something to do, then. She moved to the side window, opened it, gestured for Taylor.

The dog didn't move.

Shit.

Keeping low, she approached the dog, her arms wide. The shaking seemed to ease as she drew closer, and Taylor didn't object to being picked up. That was something. Taylor hated being picked up.

She hadn't lifted the dog in a while. She was heavier than she remembered.

It wasn't until they were almost at the window that Taylor began to writhe. Bobby tightened her grip, leaned out, and let the bundle drop from her arms onto the snow-covered ground outside.

The dog just stood there, looking up at her, a *why-do-you-hate-me* look in her big brown eyes.

"Run," said Bobby.

"Bugger off," said Freddie.

Freddie.

She walked to the cage and opened the door. Freddie just sat there staring at her.

"Go on," she said.

Freddie flapped a little, but didn't move.

"Bugger off," she said.

The bird hopped out of the cage and began flying big circles around the room, just as Bobby caught the sound of a door opening.

A weapon. Was there anything she could use?

Nothing she could see. Nothing here. Maybe upstairs?

She ran into the hall. The other one was still standing

there, still grinning, not moving a muscle as she approached. She turned and ran up the stairs, expecting a bullet in the back at any moment.

Nothing. Nothing at all.

The bedroom. She ran in, pulled the door shut, looked at the lock.

No key. There had never been a key, as far as she knew. It probably wasn't even a real lock. Not that a real lock would make much difference. They could just shoot it off, couldn't they?

She ran to the bedside table and opened the top drawer. Nothing. She heard something downstairs.

"What the—?" said a male voice.

Another voice cut him off. "Wipe your feet."

"Fuck's sake," said the first voice.

There was a moment's silence, and then a gunshot.

Even from upstairs, it was louder than she'd expected. For a moment afterward, the silence seemed more silent and still than ever before. Like the world had just stopped.

He'd shot Freddie. That *bastard* had shot Freddie.

Bobby pulled open the second drawer, trying not to think about what had just happened. Nail kit. Better than nothing. But no. The scissors weren't even there.

Where the fuck are the scissors?

It didn't matter. They wouldn't be much use against a gun.

"Bugger off," said a voice.

Bobby smiled, in spite of everything.

"Fuck's sake," repeated the man. Bobby waited for a second gunshot, but none came.

Just the gentle sound of footsteps. She could track the movement because she knew where he'd be heading. Across the living room to the hallway, where his friend would be pointing him up the stairs.

And then the staircase itself. A creak, four steps up – there it was.

She was almost spinning now, peering into the corners of the room, looking for something. For anything. The window sill. The bookcase. Her pockets.

Nothing. Just Vaseline.

She squeezed her eyes closed, forced herself to breathe slowly. She tried to think, but all she could see was Victor.

Then Miles and Stacey.

Then yesterday. At the docks. Carter's little nod. The other man watching her.

Had that been the order?

No. If that had been the order, she wouldn't have survived the night.

So what had happened? *Cummings.* It had to be Cummings.

Bugger off, Cummings.

Her eyes still closed, Bobby ran through the rest of the day, desperate for a clue, a suggestion, anything.

The coffee. Shiv. The newspaper. McKenzie. The other murder. The one at the Bridge Inn.

The one at the Bridge Inn.

She felt the smile form on her face as she moved silently to the door, pulling the Vaseline from her pocket as she went.

No lock. The door opened and she looked outside.

No sign of him yet. Still on the stairs. She opened the tin, gathered a lump of the thick, greasy jelly on two fingers, and smeared it onto the doorknob.

No lock, but still. Why make it easy?

She closed the door just as she saw the top of his head,

then a fraction of his face. Back in the room, she walked to the bookcase, picked out the biggest, heaviest hardback she could find, and smiled again as she opened it to the title page.

Underneath the title of the book was a short handwritten message. 'Enjoy your new home', it said. And underneath, the signature of the man who'd given it to her.

"Victor P."

She closed the book, ran her fingers over the words on the spine. *Bleak House*.

"Bugger off," she heard from downstairs, then the door moved. A gentle push, followed by a scrabbling sound, followed by the man's voice.

"Fuck's sake." Again.

More rattling. She watched as the doorknob began to move, but just a fraction of a turn.

Another sound. A snapping noise. Gloves coming off, she hoped.

The doorknob turned. A pause. Gloves coming back on?

It didn't matter now. She'd done all she could.

She threw the book as he entered the room, but he saw it coming, stepped smartly aside, and she watched as it sailed onto the landing.

Her gaze moved from his covered face to the gun.

Time seemed to freeze. For what felt like an eternity, nothing happened.

Silence.

The little black 'O' of the barrel, pointing at her face. In the movie she'd been watching, the villain had survived bullet after bullet.

But that was just a movie.

There was a noise from outside.

Just the wind?

She waited. *No.* An engine.

Another car.

Her eyes moved back up. She could see his eyes. See them widen as he heard it, too.

It was a long way, up the track to the house. Whoever it was, they wouldn't be there for a while.

But still. Someone was coming. She was about to die, but he might not have time to wipe away the traces.

They were smart, Aaron Keyes and his mates.

Bobby Silver closed her eyes and smiled.

"Here's to you, Victor," she said, but her words were lost to the sound of the bullet.

READ ON FOR THE MYRON CARTER CASE FILE...

Want to know more about the current status of the investigation into Myron Carter's activities?
Read on for Zoe's case file...

CUMBRIA POLICE - CASE FILE

Case Number: [To be assigned]
Case Title: Investigation into Myron Carter
Lead Investigator: DI Zoe Finch

Persons Involved:

- Myron Carter – Suspect
- DI Zoe Finch – Lead Investigator
- DS Aaron Keyes – Investigating Officer
- DC Tom Willis – Investigating Officer
- DC Nina Kapoor – Investigating Officer
- DCI Carl Whaley – Professional Standards Division
- DS Denise Gaskill – Professional Standards Division
- DI Ralph Streeting – Suspected Corrupt Officer
- Victor Parlick – Deceased, involved in organised crime
- Elena Marin – Trafficking Victim and Witness

- Olivia Bagsby – Artist, Witness
- DC Harriett Barnes (undercover as PC Harriett Barnes) – Professional Standards Division

Background:

The investigation into Myron Carter centres on his involvement in organised crime, specifically human trafficking and modern slavery. It is suspected that Carter is a key figure in a network that traffics women into the UK, using them in brothels and other areas of the unregulated and undocumented workforce economy.

Key Findings:

1. **Photographic Evidence**:
    - Photographs taken by Olivia Bagsby at the port show Myron Carter shouting at DI Ralph Streeting. Another figure, identified as Victor Parlick, is seen in a later shot.
    - A second set of photos shows a group of women, suspected trafficking victims, being marched past DI Streeting, with Carter not present in those photos.
2. **Witness Testimonies**:
    - **Elena Marin**: Escaped trafficking victim who provided limited details but remembered being held in a warehouse with a strong ammonia smell. Currently staying with DC Nina Kapoor.
    - **Victor Parlick**: Had provided intel about Carter's empire before being found dead.

- **Carrie Wright**: Formerly Sergeant Carrie Wright, under investigation and awaiting trial for drug and misconduct charges. Provided information linking blackmail and operational details to the greater crime network but provided no specific names.

3. **Financial Investigation**:
    - Utilizing SSD Zhang Chen, a forensic accountant, DI Finch's team traced payments through offshore companies connected to Carter. Clear linkage to local organized crime, yet more direct evidence of Carter's personal involvement needed.

4. **Key Incidents**:
    - **Carrie Wright's Arrest**: Revealed a network using blackmail to control police officers, drug dealers and civilians alike, operating without Carter's consent and targeting his supply.
    - **Joshua McKenzie's Murder**: Investigated due to his connections and involvement in the criminal network. Reviewing his connections has proven vital.
    - **PC Cumming's Arrest**: Revealed a further link between criminal gangs and the police, and a direct connection with McKenzie.

Current Hypotheses:

- DI Ralph Streeting is believed to be complicit in Carter's operations, possibly under duress or through active willingness.
- Carter's trafficking operation involves the importation of women into the UK, holding them in locations such as the warehouses close to the paper mill in Workington (see below).
- Bobby Silver's murder (see below) was orchestrated by Carter and Streeting following an inadvertent tipoff of Silver's identity.

Pending Actions:

- **Interviews/Re-interviews:**
    - Re-interviewing relevant parties with new evidence.
    - Pursuing deeper financial audits on identified Carter-associated companies.
- **Surveillance:**
    - Continuation of surveillance on identified affiliated sites such as the paper mill in Workington.
- **Further Investigation:**
    - Efforts to secure actionable evidence against Carter, including through former Carter employee Ryan Tobin, and to confirm the role and extent of DI Streeting's complicity.

Recent Developments:

- **Bobby Silver's Death**: The murder of the leading figure in the McKenzie/Cummings network is believed to have been carried out on Carter's orders, highlighting the immediate danger and reach of the criminal network.
- Confirmation of the ammonia smell linked to the potential holding area for the trafficked women at the Workington paper mill area.

Conclusion:

The investigation has strong circumstantial evidence linking Myron Carter to a widespread human trafficking operation with multiple associated crimes including murder, blackmail, and corruption within the police force. Efforts are ongoing to gather sufficient evidence to prosecute Carter and uncover his entire network of operations.

Next Steps:

- Gather definite evidence to formally charge Myron Carter.
- Protect and assist witnesses who can provide further evidence.
- Close gaps in the financial paper trail linked to Carter's operations.
- Bring DI Ralph Streeting to justice upon securing evidence of his complicity.

Attachments:

- Photographs
- Witness Statements
- Financial Records
- Surveillance Reports

Submitted by: DI Zoe Finch

Date: January 2025

CUMBRIA CRIME BOOK 6, THE WOOD

DI Zoe Finch has been in Cumbria long enough to know who's pulling the strings in organised crime, and who's helping them from within the police.

But just as she's closing in on the evidence to prove it, she finds herself scrambling in the fallout from the murder of a key witness, and struggling to keep the case out of the hands of the very man she suspects of orchestrating it.

Can the women rescued from a human trafficking ring help Zoe wrest back control of the investigation? And does a seemingly unrelated murder on the other side of the Lake District hold the key to bringing her enemies to justice?

With the team thrust into unfamiliar roles and the whole station under investigation, the stakes have never been higher. Can Zoe and her team hold it together under mounting pressure?

Buy from book retailers or via the Rachel McLean website.

READ THE CUMBRIA CRIME SERIES

The Harbour

The Mine

The Cairn

The Barn

The Lake

The Wood

...and more to come

Buy from book retailers or via the Rachel McLean website.

ALSO BY RACHEL MCLEAN

The DI Zoe Finch Series – buy from book retailers or via the Rachel McLean website.

Deadly Wishes

Deadly Choices

Deadly Desires

Deadly Terror

Deadly Reprisal

Deadly Fallout

Deadly Christmas

Deadly Origins, the FREE Zoe Finch prequel

The Dorset Crime Series – buy from book retailers or via the Rachel McLean website.

The Corfe Castle Murders

The Clifftop Murders

The Island Murders

The Monument Murders

The Millionaire Murders

The Fossil Beach Murders

The Blue Pool Murders

The Lighthouse Murders

The Ghost Village Murders

The Poole Harbour Murders

...and more to com

The McBride & Tanner Series – buy from book retailers or via the Rachel McLean website.

Blood and Money

Death and Poetry

Power and Treachery

Secrets and History

The London Cosy Mystery Series by Rachel McLean and Millie Ravensworth – buy from book retailers or via the Rachel McLean website.

Death at Westminster

Death in the West End

Death at Tower Bridge

Death on the Thames

Death at St Paul's Cathedral

Death at Abbey Road

The Lyme Regis Women's Swimming Club series by Rachel McLean and Millie Ravensworth – buy from book retailers or via the Rachel McLean website.

The Lyme Regis Women's Swimming Club

...and more to come

ALSO BY JOEL HAMES

The Sam Williams Series – Buy now in ebook, paperback and audiobook

Dead North

No One Will Hear

The Cold Years

The Art of Staying Dead

Victims, a Sam Williams novella

Caged, a Sam Williams short

Printed and bound by CPI Group (UK) Ltd, Croydon, CR0 4YY
11/12/2025
02017243-0002